This book belongs to

_____

Based on the TV series *Dora the Explorer* ® and *Go, Diego, Go!* ™ as seen on Nick Jr.®

SIMON SPOTLIGHT
An imprint of Simon & Schuster Children's Publishing Division
1230 Avenue of the Americas, New York, New York 10020
Diego's Wolf Pup Rescue, Dora's World Adventure!, and *A Humpback Whale Tale* © 2006 Viacom International Inc.
Dora Climbs Star Mountain, Dora Saves Mermaid Kingdom, and *Diego's Safari Rescue* © 2007 Viacom International Inc;
Diego's Springtime Fiesta © 2008 Viacom International Inc.

Manufactured in China
4 6 8 10 9 7 5 3
ISBN-13: 978-1-4169-7093-4
ISBN-10: 1-4169-7093-2
These titles were previously published individually by Simon Spotlight.
0410 SCP

NICKELODEON

Storytime

WITH DORA AND DIEGO

Simon Spotlight/Nickelodeon

New York   London   Toronto   Sydney

Contents

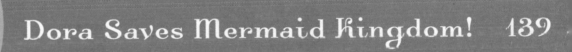

Diego's Springtime Fiesta

by Lara Bergen
illustrated by Brian Oesch

¡Hola! Soy Diego. I'm an Animal Rescuer. But today I'm getting the Animal Rescue Center ready for the big Springtime Fiesta! Do you like fiestas? Me too! I can't wait! I'm taking my Rescue Truck back to the Animal Rescue Center now. Come on!

¡Mira! Look! It's a mother cottontail rabbit. She has a big pile of cactus fruits for her family to eat at the Springtime Fiesta. How many does she have? Let's count. *Uno, dos, tres, cuatro, cinco.*

She has five cactus fruits! She must have five babies to feed. But where are her baby bunnies?

I see the rabbit's nest, which is lined with grass and soft fur. But it's empty. Oh, no! The baby bunnies are missing. Let's help Mommy Rabbit find them!

Don't worry, Mommy Rabbit. We'll help you find your bunnies!

15

My Field Journal tells me that rabbits leave their nests to go explore or look for food. Maybe the baby bunnies did that too!

Look! There are five trails in this tall grass. Do you think they were made by the baby bunnies? Let's go check it out!

A rabbit's fur helps it blend in with the grass, so we have to look carefully for the bunnies. Do you see a baby bunny in this tall grass?

¡Sí! There he is! We found you, Baby Bunny!

The baby bunny says that he was searching for leaves to decorate the Springtime Fiesta when he lost his way. We're glad we found you, Baby Bunny. The leaves you gathered are perfect for the party!

19

Rabbits love to eat grass and leaves on trees and bushes. Do you see any plants around here that a baby bunny might have nibbled? *¡Allí esta!* Over there! And there's the second baby bunny! She's stuck behind those branches!

Don't worry, Baby Bunny. We'll move those branches and get you out! The baby bunny says she was searching for yummy treats for the Springtime Fiesta when she got stuck. You're safe now, Baby Bunny.

My Field Journal tells me that rabbit tracks look like this. Do you see any rabbit tracks in this muddy riverbank? Which way did the baby bunny go?

¡Sí! The baby bunny went this way to the stream to get a cool drink. But look! He is stuck on a log that fell into the stream!

Don't worry, Baby Bunny. Rescue Pack can transform into a raft. Now we can paddle to you! ¡Al rescate! To the rescue! We've got you, Baby Bunny.

We have saved three baby bunnies.
How many more do we need to find?
¡Sí! Two! Do you see another baby
bunny? There he is, under that log. He is being
very still. He must be hiding from something.

What is he hiding from? *¡Sí!* The gray hawk! Rabbits are afraid of hawks.

Let's be still like rabbits until the hawk flies away.

Uno, dos, tres, cuatro. We found four baby rabbits. But there is still one more trail to follow! Let's find the last bunny.

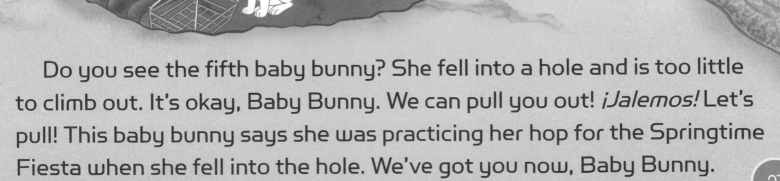

Do you see the fifth baby bunny? She fell into a hole and is too little to climb out. It's okay, Baby Bunny. We can pull you out! *¡Jalemos!* Let's pull! This baby bunny says she was practicing her hop for the Springtime Fiesta when she fell into the hole. We've got you now, Baby Bunny.

Let's count the bunnies to make sure they are all here. *Uno, dos, tres, cuatro, cinco.* All five baby bunnies are safe!

Now let's take them back to their mommy.

Mommy Rabbit is so happy to have her family together again! Let's all go to the Springtime Fiesta at the Animal Rescue Center. *¡Fantástico!* We can hop in my Rescue Truck to get there.

We made it to the Animal Rescue Center for the Springtime Fiesta—with our flowers and our new rabbit friends, too! *¡Misión cumplida!* Springtime mission complete!

Dora Climbs Star Mountain

adapted by Alison Inches
illustrated by A&J Studios

¡Hola! I'm Dora, and this is my best friend, Boots. Today I got a present from my grandma. *Mi abuela* made me a necklace to match my bracelet. I really love it! Do you like presents too?

Uh-oh, that sounds like Swiper the Fox! That sneaky fox will try to swipe my necklace. If you see Swiper, say "Swiper, no . . ."

Oh, no! We're too late. Swiper swiped my necklace and threw it to the top of Star Mountain. I really love my necklace. Will you help Boots and me get it back? Great!

Star Mountain is where the Explorer Stars live. If we call them, they will help us find my necklace. To call the Explorer Stars, we have to say *"Estrellas."* Say it with us. *"¡Estrellas!"*

Look! The Explorer Stars came! There's Tool Star, the Explorer Star with lots of tools. And there is Saltador, the super jumping Explorer Star. And there is Glowy, the bright light Explorer Star. The Explorer Stars will help us get my necklace back.

First we have to figure out how to get to the top of Star Mountain. Who do we ask for help when we don't know which way to go? Map! Say "Map!"

Map says that to get my necklace back, we have to run up fifteen steps. Then we have to climb all the way up the Diamond. And that's how we'll get to the Giant Star on top of Star Mountain.

Do you see the steps? *¿Dónde están?* There they are! But they're covered in fog! We need Tool Star to help us through the fog. Which tool can Tool Star use to get us through the fog? *¡Sí!* A fan!

Tool Star is fanning the fog out of the way. Good fanning!

We made it through the fog to the steps. Count the fifteen steps with me. *Uno, dos, tres, cuatro, cinco, seis, siete, ocho, nueve, diez, once, doce, trece, catorce, quince.*

Great counting! We made it up all fifteen steps. But look at all this bubbling green goo! It's blocking our way! We need an Explorer Star to help us get past this goo. Glowy, the bright light Star, can help us melt the goo with her hot lights. Go, Glowy!

Yay! We made it past the goo! So where do we go next? Yeah, the Diamond! Wait, I hear a rumbling sound. It's a giant rock!

Look! It's Saltador, the super jumping Explorer Star. Saltador can help us jump over the falling rock. Let's jump on the count of three. Count with me. *¡Uno, dos, TRES!* We jumped over the giant rock! *¡Gracias, Saltador!*

Now let's use these star handles to climb the Diamond. The stars are red and green, *roja y verde*. We have to follow the pattern to climb to the top. Will you help? Say *"¡Roja! ¡Verde! ¡Roja! ¡Verde!"* Good job!

We made it up the Diamond! Thanks for helping. Now we need to go to the Giant Star to get my necklace back. *¿Dónde está?*

There's the Giant Star! And there's my necklace! To get up the Giant Star, we're going to need a long rope. Will you check Backpack for a long rope? You have to say "Backpack!"

Do you see a long rope? *¡Muy bien!* Very good! Thanks!

53

Now I have to throw the rope to the top of the Giant Star.
Wish me luck! Say *"¡Buena suerte!"*
Wow, I did it! Thanks for your help!

Now I have to grab the rope and climb to the top. Will you help me climb? Say *"¡Sube! ¡Sube, sube, sube!"* Great climbing! Do you see my necklace?

I see it! My necklace! My necklace!

¡Lo hicimos! We did it! You helped me get back my necklace, and the Explorer Stars helped too. *¡Gracias, estrellas!*

I couldn't have done it without you. *¡Gracias!* Thanks for helping!

Diego's Wolf Pup Rescue

adapted by Christine Ricci

based on the original teleplay by Valerie Walsh

illustrated by Art Mawhinney

"We're Animal Rescuers!" shouted Diego as he slid down the pole from the Animal Rescue Center's observation platform.

"Animal Rescuers!" chanted his cousin Dora as she followed Diego down the pole.

Dora was visiting the Animal Rescue Center, and Diego had a special surprise for her.

"Watch this!" said Diego as he cupped his hand to his mouth and called, "Ah-ruff! Ah-ruff!"

Suddenly several maned wolf pups poked their heads out of the tall grass. *"Ah-ruff! Ah-ruff!"* they barked.

"Maned wolf pups!" said Dora excitedly. "What a great surprise!"

The pups playfully scampered over to Diego and Dora.

"They're so small!" giggled Dora as the pups climbed on her.

"And this one is the littlest," said Diego as he stroked the tiny pup's fur.

Just then Diego's sister Alicia arrived with Mommy Maned Wolf. "Mommy Maned Wolf came to the Rescue Center to have her wolf pups," Alicia explained.

Dora turned to Mommy Maned Wolf. "Your little pups are so cute. And there are so many of them!"

"Maned wolves can have up to five pups at a time," Mommy Maned Wolf said proudly.

"How many pups are there?" asked Diego. "Let's count them."

Dora and Diego counted the wolf pups: one, two, three, four. Four maned wolf pups!

Mommy Maned Wolf gasped. "Only *four* maned wolf pups?" she asked. "But I have *five* pups! My littlest pup is missing!"

"Don't worry, Mommy Maned Wolf!" said Diego. "We're Animal Rescuers. We'll find your littlest pup."

Alicia decided to stay at the Animal Rescue Center to help Mommy Maned Wolf with the other pups. "Go, Animal Rescuers! Go!" she cheered as Diego and Dora ran off toward the Science Deck.

Diego and Dora ran over to their special camera, Click.
"Click can help us find the baby maned wolf," said Diego.

Click zoomed through the forest and found the little wolf pup.

"He's heading for the prickers and thorns!" said Diego, watching closely. "He could get hurt."

"We've got to rescue him!" said Dora.

"*¡Al rescate!*" shouted Diego. "To the rescue!"

Diego and Dora jumped on a zip cord and zoomed through the forest. They landed at a fork in the road. "Look!" said Diego. "There are prints on each path."

"But which ones belong to the baby maned wolf?" Dora asked.

Diego pulled out his Field Journal and scrolled to a picture of a maned wolf's paw print. "Which path has prints that look like these?" he asked.

"These prints match," exclaimed Dora as she pointed to the third path. "*¡Vámonos!* Let's go!"

The path led them to a river. Diego pulled out his spotting scope and located the wolf pup's prints on the far bank. "We need to get across this river to keep following the wolf pup's tracks," said Diego.

"I can help!" called out Rescue Pack.

"Me too!" chimed in Backpack.

Rescue Pack and Backpack worked together to help get Diego and Dora across the river. Rescue Pack transformed himself into a raft. Backpack gave them paddles and a life jacket.

After turning his vest into a second life jacket, Diego jumped into the raft next to Dora. They started to paddle down the river. Suddenly Diego noticed a river otter stuck in a whirlpool. "We have to rescue the river otter!" he shouted.

Diego threw a life preserver to the river otter, and the river otter scrambled onto it. Then Diego and Dora pulled the river otter to safety.

"Thanks for rescuing me," said the river otter.

"We're Animal Rescuers," replied Diego. "It's what we do!"

Once on shore Diego and Dora ran toward the prickers and thorns. But when they arrived, the little maned wolf was nowhere in sight. Diego cupped his hands to his ears to listen for the pup. Finally he heard a bark.

"Ah-ruff!"

"It sounds like he's in these bushes," said Diego.

Diego and Dora stretched up tall to see over the pricker and thorn bushes.

The little maned wolf was heading toward a sharp prickly bush!
"Stop, Baby Maned Wolf!" called Diego and Dora. "Stop!"
Baby Maned Wolf heard the warning and stopped right in front of the sharp prickly bush.

Diego and Dora ran over to the little wolf pup and knelt down next to him.

"Hi, Baby Maned Wolf!" Diego said. "We're Animal Rescuers! You're safe now!"

"Thanks for rescuing me," said Baby Maned Wolf. "I can't wait to see my Mommy and my brothers and sisters."

Back at the Animal Rescue Center, Mommy Maned Wolf nuzzled her littlest pup and made sure he wasn't hurt. Baby Maned Wolf was so happy to be with his family that he jumped into Diego's arms and gave him a big lick on the cheek.

Then Baby Maned Wolf curled up next to the other pups and fell fast asleep.

"*¡Misión cumplida!* Rescue complete!" whispered Diego. "That was a great animal adventure!"

Did you know?

The MANE event!

The maned wolf is called maned because it grows a mane of long black hair on its back.

A leg up!

Maned wolves live in grasslands and swampy areas. The maned wolf's long legs allow it to see over tall grass.

Howl are you?

Maned wolves talk to each other by howling.

My, what big ears you have!

Maned wolves can rotate their large ears to listen for other animals. They have excellent hearing!

Dora's WORLD ADVENTURE!™

adapted by Suzanne D. Nimm
based on the teleplay written by Valerie Walsh
illustrated by Tom Mangano

¡Hola! I'm Dora! Today is Friendship Day: ¡El Día de la Amistad! On Friendship Day friends around the world have parties and wear special friendship bracelets. If we wear our bracelets, we'll all be friends forever and ever! Do you want to see the friendship bracelets?

The friendship bracelets are so beautiful!
Oh, no! There's Swiper, and he's trying to swipe our friendship bracelets! Let's stop Swiper from swiping our bracelets. Say "Swiper, no swiping!"

Look! Swiper has been swiping bracelets from all
around the world. But he didn't know they were special
friendship bracelets. There won't be a Friendship Day
unless everyone has a friendship bracelet, Swiper! We
need to return them!

Swiper and I are going to travel around the world and return the bracelets to all our friends for Friendship Day. Will you come with us? Great!

Who do we ask for help when we don't know which way to go? Yeah, Map!

Map says that to return the friendship bracelets to our friends, we have to go to the Eiffel Tower in France, to Mount Kilimanjaro in Tanzania, to the Winter Palace in Russia, and to the Great Wall of China.

¡Vámonos! Let's go around the world!

We're in France! And this is my friend Amelie! To say "hello" to Amelie in French, we say "bonjour." Let's say "bonjour" to Amelie. Bonjour, Amelie!

Amelie is going to help us bring the bracelets back to the Eiffel Tower.

Amelie says that the smiling gargoyle will help us find the Eiffel Tower. There's the smiling gargoyle! The smiling gargoyle says that we need to follow the street with the diamond stones. Do you see the diamond stones? Great! We'll go that way!

Yay! Swiper is giving everyone at the Eiffel Tower their friendship bracelets! Oh, no! Fifi the skunk is sneaking up on Swiper. Fifi will try to swipe the bracelets. Help me stop Fifi! Say "Fifi, no swiping!"

Hooray! We stopped Fifi! Now all our friends
in France have friendship bracelets.
There are many more bracelets to return.
¡Vámonos! Let's go!

97

We made it to Tanzania. This is my friend N'Dari. To say "hello" to N'Dari, we say "jambo." N'Dari says that everyone is waiting for the friendship bracelets at Mount Kilimanjaro.

Quick, we have to take a safari ride to the mountain! Along the way we have to watch out for wild animals. How many zebras, lions, giraffes, hippos, and elephants do you see?

Hmm! I think I hear another wild animal. It sounds like a hyena. Do you see a hyena?

That's Sami the hyena! He's going to try to swipe the bracelets. Will you help me stop Sami? Say "Sami, no swiping!"

Yay! We stopped Sami! Come on, everyone! Come and get your friendship bracelets!

Now we have to bring the friendship bracelets to the Winter Palace in Russia. Do you see something that can fly us there? The hot-air balloon! Great idea!

We made it to Russia! But the Troll won't let us inside the Winter Palace.

My friend Vladimir can help us. Vladimir says the Troll will open the gate if we make him laugh. Let's make silly faces to get the Troll to laugh! Make a silly face!

What great silly faces!

Our silly faces made the Troll laugh, and he opened the gate! And look! The Winter Palace is filled with lots of friends! Let's say "hello" to everyone. In Russian we say "preevyet!"

The children decorated the Winter Palace for Friendship Day! There are icicles, balloons, flags, snowmen, and even a dancing bear!

Fom-kah the bear is very sneaky. He's going to try to swipe the friendship bracelets. Help us stop Fomkah. Say "Fom-kah, no swiping!"

Yay! We stopped Fom-kah! Now we can return the friendship bracelets to our friends in Russia.

We have more bracelets to return. *¡Vámonos!*

We made it to the Great Wall of China. Wow! What a party! But we have to make sure these bracelets stay safe. Watch out for Ying Ying the weasel. If you see him, say "Ying Ying, no swiping!"

This is my friend Mei. To say "hello" to Mei, we say "knee-how." Mei is helping us give out the friendship bracelets.

Hooray! We returned all the friendship bracelets. Now we can start the Friendship Day celebration!

We made it back home for our Friendship Day celebration. We have eight friendship bracelets left. How many friends are at our party? *¡Siete!* Seven! They all get a friendship bracelet.

And there's one more bracelet! It's a friendship
bracelet for you—because you're such a great friend!

Wow! The bracelets are glowing! Rainbow sparkles are lighting the sky all over the world! Thanks for helping us save Friendship Day! Now we'll all be friends forever and ever! We did it! —

A Humpback Whale Tale

adapted by Justin Spelvin

based on the original teleplay by Chris Gifford and Val Walsh

illustrated by Ron Zalme

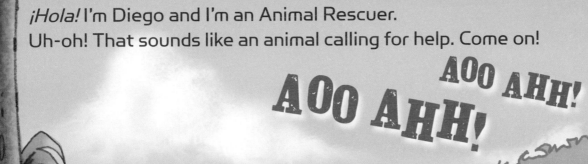

¡Hola! I'm Diego and I'm an Animal Rescuer.
Uh-oh! That sounds like an animal calling for help. Come on!

AOO AHH!

AOO AHH!

AOO AHH!

First we need to find out who's in trouble. Click the Camera can help. Say "Click!" Click has four pictures of animals. The animal that needs our help says "Aoo ahh, aoo ahh." Do you see an animal like that?

¡Sí! The humpback whale. When humpback whales dive underwater, they bend their backs in a hump shape. But this baby whale is stuck on a rocky island all by himself. We've got to save the baby humpback whale and get him back to his mommy!

¡Al rescate, mis amigos! To the rescue, my friends!

We have to get through these swinging vines without getting tangled in them. Let's bend our backs like humpback whales to go under the vines. Watch out for spiders and snakes!

Great bending! We've got to call to the baby humpback whale to let him know we're coming. Call with me. "Aoo ahh! Aoo ahh!"

Now we need to find the path that leads to the beach. Let's think like scientists. Should we take the path that goes toward the rainforest, toward the mountain, or toward the ocean?

Yeah, this is the path that leads to the beach! We're almost there, but we can't walk on these sand dunes. They are here to protect the beach. We need something to help us fly over them. I know! Rescue Pack can transform into anything I need. Say "¡Activate!"

What do we need to fly over the dunes?

125

A hot-air balloon! *¡Perfecto!*
Oh, no! It's the Bobo Brothers. Those silly monkeys are always causing trouble.
If they keep bouncing on our balloon, we'll never get to the baby humpback whale!

To stop the Bobos we have to clap three times.
Now say "Freeze, Bobos!"

Uh-oh, look! Giant, stinging jellyfish! The jellyfish could sting us, but we've got to get to that whale!

Hey! We can ask my friend Tuga the Leatherback Sea Turtle if we can ride on her back. Jellyfish are scared of leatherback sea turtles.

Tuga speaks Spanish, so to tell Tuga that we need to swim, say *"¡Nademos!"*
Uh-oh! We're being chased by sharks! We'd better swim even faster. *¡Nademos!*
¡Nademos!

We made it! This baby humpback whale needs to get back in the water fast. We can't lift him off the island, but maybe a big wave can.

Humpback whales make really big waves when they splash their tails in the water. Let's call for the humpback whale family to help us make really big waves. Say "Aoo ahh! Aoo ahh!"

AOO AHH!

Splash, whales, splash!
Look, the big wave is carrying the baby humpback whale back to his mommy!

¡Excellente! We did it! The baby humpback whale is back safe with his family.
¡Mision cumplida! Rescue complete! You're a great Animal Rescuer!

Did you know?

Nice trick!

Humpback whales are the ocean's acrobats. They jump completely out of the water and land on their backs with a terrific splash!

Tiny appetites!

Even though they are so big, humpback whales eat only small fish, and tiny plants and animals.

Long and strong!

Most grown-up humpback whales are about forty feet long. That's about the size of a school bus!

Sweet tunes!

Male humpback whales communicate to female humpback whales by singing.

Tipping the scales!

A fully grown humpback whale weighs about as much as four elephants.

Dora Saves
MERMAID KINGDOM!

adapted by Michael Teitelbaum
based on the original teleplay by Valerie Walsh
illustrated by Artful Doodlers

¡Hola! I'm Dora, and this is my best friend, Boots. We love the beach. We love the ocean, the warm sand, the bright blue sky, and the sunny sun.

Today is Clean-Up-the-Beach Day! That's when we make sure the beach is nice and clean!

Let's pick up all the garbage and put it in the garbage bag. Do you see any garbage on the beach? *¡Sí!* There's a juice box! And there's a food wrapper!

¿Qué más? What else do you see? If you see more garbage, say "¡Basura!"

¡Mira! There is a big clam on the beach. To tell the big clam to open, say "*¡Abre!*"

Great job! This big clam has
a special story to tell us.

The clam's story is about the Mermaid Kingdom.

146

Once upon a time a mean octopus dumped garbage all over the Mermaid Kingdom. Luckily, a mermaid named Mariana found a magic crown so she could wish all the garbage away. But a wave washed away Mariana's magic crown, and now she can't stop the mean octopus!

We need to help Mariana and the Mermaid Kingdom by finding that magic crown. Where could it be?

If you see the crown, say *"¡Corona!"* Do you see the magic crown? There it is!

Now we can bring the crown back to Mariana! Let's find the Mermaid Kingdom! Who do we ask for help when we don't know which way to go?

¡Sí! Map! Say "Map!"

Map says that we have to cross the Seashell Bridge and then go through Pirate Island to get to the Silly Sea. That's where we will find the Mermaid Kingdom. Come on! *¡Vámonos!*

We made it to the Seashell Bridge, but we can't get across! That mean octopus has covered the bridge with garbage. Let's look inside Backpack for something to clean up the bridge. Say "Backpack!"

Is there anything in Backpack that we can use to clean up the bridge?

¡Si! A vacuum cleaner!

Now that we cleaned Seashell Bridge, we can get across. Let's count the shells as we cross. *Uno, dos, tres, cuatro, cinco, seis.* One, two, three, four, five, six.

3

5

2

4

6

1

¡Gracias! Thanks for helping us cross the bridge.

We made it to Pirate Island, but the Coconut Trees are in our way.

The Pirate Piggies show us how to do the Coconut Conga to get past the trees. Ready?
Wiggle, wiggle, wiggle!

Now we need to cross the Silly Sea. Look at all these Silly Sea animals. Who can help us swim past them all and through the Silly Sea? Yeah, dolphins!

My cousin Diego can help us call the dolphins.
To help Diego call the dolphins, we need to say "Squeak, squeak!"

We made it to the Mermaid Kingdom! Let's give Mariana back her magic crown so she can clean up the Mermaid Kingdom.

Oh, no! We're too late! The octopus threw a big net over Mariana. Now she's trapped!

Ooooh! Mariana gave me the crown just in time! I put it on, and now I'm a mermaid! *¡Fantástico!*

The magic crown lets me have one wish. What should we wish for?

Let's wish to clean up the Mermaid Kingdom. Ready? I wish to clean up the Mermaid Kingdom!

There is still garbage in the kingdom! We're going to need help from our ocean friends!
Say "Clean-up time!"
¡Excelente! Mermaid Kingdom is getting clean.

Now we have to rescue Mariana. *¡Vámonos!*
Let's pull the net off of Mariana. *¡Muy bien!* Now she is free!

¡Mira! The net fell on the octopus, and he has fallen in the garbage.

The octopus promises to put all garbage in the garbage dump from now on, instead of on the Mermaid Kingdom! Hooray! *¡Lo hicimos!* We did it!

Mariana needs her crown back, but she gave me a magical mermaid necklace so I can visit her anytime.

I know that we'll be friends forever, just like you and me! Thanks for helping me save Mariana and the Mermaid Kingdom! I couldn't have done it without you.

Diego's
Safari Rescue

adapted by Ligiah Villalobos
based on the original teleplay by Ligiah Villalobos
illustrated by Alex Maher

¡Hola! I'm Diego. I'm an Animal Rescuer. This is my sister Alicia, and this is Baby Jaguar. We're visiting the Serengeti in Africa to help our friend Juma rescue the elephants!

Juma says that a long time ago, the Serengeti in Africa had lots and lots of elephants. Do you see all of the elephants? *¡Sí!* There they are. All of the animals loved the elephants—except for one mosquito who found a magic wand and changed herself into a magician.

The magician didn't like elephants, so she used her magic wand to turn them into giant rocks!

Juma says there's a magic drum that can break the magician's spell. It's hidden in a cave on top of the tallest mountain. Do you see the tallest mountain? ¡Sí! That's the tallest mountain. And there's the cave.

We'll need something that can get us to the top of that mountain. Who can help? Rescue Pack! To activate Rescue Pack, say "¡Actívate!"

Rescue Pack can transform into anything we need: a boat, roller skates, or a hot-air balloon. What can fly us all the way to the top of the tallest mountain? *¡Sí!* A hot-air balloon!

Rescue Pack transformed into a hot-air balloon. *Bien hecho*, Rescue Pack! Now we can go find the magic drum! Come on!

We made it to the cave. And look! There's an elephant! Her name is Erin. She says she came to the cave to hide from the magician and protect the magic drum. Do you see the magic drum? *¡Sí!* There it is!

Now that we've found the magic drum, we can go rescue the elephants who turned into rocks! Our special camera, Click, will help us find out where they are. Say "Click!"

Click says we'll have to go through the dry forest and across the lake to get to the giant rocks so we can break the spell and rescue the elephants. *¡Al rescate!* To the rescue!

We made it to the dry forest, but the trees are blocking our way. Erin the Elephant says she can use her trunk to pull the trees out of the way. Elephants have superstrong trunks!

Will you help Erin the Elephant pull the trees out of the way? Great! Make elephant trunks with your arms, and pull, pull, pull!

Great job pulling like an elephant. Now the trees aren't blocking our way! And look! Do you see the giraffes? They look different, don't they? *¡Sí!* The magician made their necks really short.

Juma says that maybe the magic drum can help us make their necks long again. Will you beat the magic drum with us? *¡Excelente!* Put your hands out in front of you, and drum, drum, drum!

It worked! The magic drum made the giraffes' necks long again! The giraffes say thank you. Let's keep going so we can rescue the elephants!

Uh-oh! I hear a lion roaring! Alicia says that elephants are afraid of lions. But elephants can scare away lions by stomping their feet very loudly. Let's help Erin the Elephant scare away the lion. Stomp with your feet! Stomp, stomp, stomp!

Yay! We helped Erin the Elephant scare away the lion. And we made it to the lake. The lake is very deep, but we've got to find a way to get across it!

Erin the Elephant says elephants love to swim. She says she can get us across! Will you help Erin the Elephant swim across the lake? *¡Excelente!* Put your arms out in front of you, and swim, swim, swim!

We made it across the lake. *¡Gracias!* Thanks for helping!

Hey, look! Do you see the zebras and hippos? Do they look different? *¡Sí!* The magician took away the zebras' stripes and made the hippos really small.

Juma thinks the magic drum can help them. Let's beat the magic drum! Put your hands out in front of you, and drum, drum, drum!

The magic drum worked! The zebras got their stripes back, and the hippos are big again! Let's keep going so we can break the spell and save all of the elephants.

We made it to the rocks. Those are the elephants we need to save! Oh, no! There's the magician! She turned Erin the Elephant into a rock!

We've got to use the magic drum to unfreeze all of the elephants! Drum with us! Put your hands out in front of you, and drum, drum, drum!

Hooray! We turned the rocks back into elephants!

185

Let's use Rescue Rope to lasso the magic wand away from the magician. Great!

The magician turned into a mosquito.

The mosquito says she missed being a mosquito and will never do mean things again. Look! She's flying away!

Erin the Elephant says she's so happy to see all of her elephant friends again! *¡Misión cumplida!* Rescue complete! You are great at rescuing animals! *¡Hasta luego!* See you soon!

Did you know?

Big, Big, Big!

Elephants are the biggest land animals in all of Africa. They're as heavy as twelve pick-up trucks!

Clean-up Time

Elephants can fill up their trunks with water and then squirt their backs with it! It's an easy way to take a quick shower!

Fast Going

Elephants are very big, but it doesn't slow them down. They can run really fast!

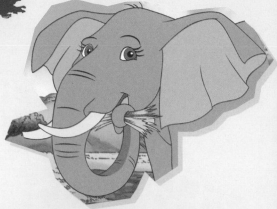

Elephants love to eat lots of things, like tree branches, fruit, and grass. They spend up to sixteen hours a day looking for food because they're hungry all the time!

Ear Fans

Elephants have big, flat ears that they flap back and forth and use like fans to cool off!